ANYA of MAJADON

ANYA of MAJADON

The Battle in Shadow Forest

to Carolyn,
My dear friend & sister in
Christ. God bless you in your
continued life's journey.
Love,
Debby
2019

Deborah Thomas

Anya of Majadon:
The Battle in Shadow Forest

© 2019 Deborah Thomas

Sun and Moon Press
Tucson, AZ

Authored and illustrated by Deborah Thomas

Front cover design: Monty Kugler
Back cover & interior design: Benjamin Vrbicek (benjaminvrbicek.com)

Trade Paperback ISBN: 978-1-7338571-0-9
Ebook ISBN: 978-1-7338571-1-6

To Rebecca M. Parker and Michelle E. Bergesen, who made my life better than any fairy tale could ever be. I count it all joy to be your mother.

CONTENTS

CHAPTER ONE

Once upon a time, in the beautiful land of Majadon lived a great king and his wife. He was King Gregory Defender of Men and she was Queen Sasha the Watchful.

The royal castle stood tall in the capital city of Majadonia, on the Otohosk Sea. It was surrounded by walls with battlements, and in its four towers, guards kept watch day and night.

Majadon had many villages. Drammend was the nearest to the capital, a day's ride, by horse. Bodo was the farthest. It was a three-day ride. The longest road connected Bodo to the capital, and it was called the King's Highway, because it was patrolled by his army.

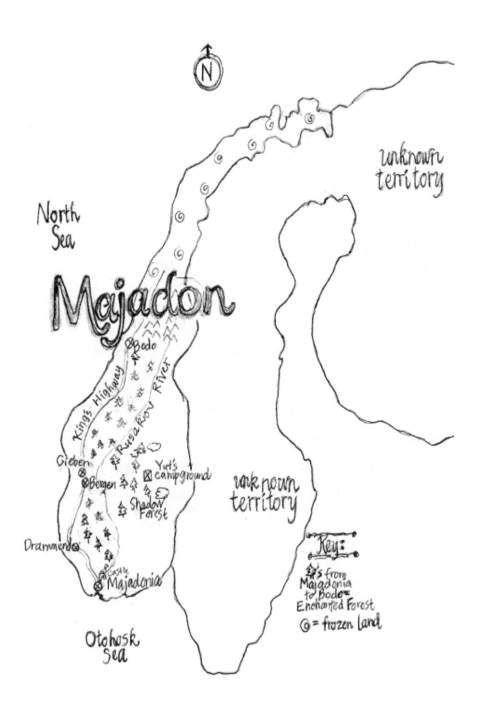

The Enchanted Forest was in east Majadon, plush and long. It held hundreds of cottages. Through the middle of it ran the Rusakov River, all the way from Bodo down to Majadonia. There, it emptied into the Okohosk Sea.

The far eastern part of the forest—Shadow Forest—was rarely entered. You had to cross the deep and wild Rusakov River to reach it.

To the west of King's Highway, The Enchanted Forest continued, but not as thick as the eastern sector. Its trees and bushes dotted the hills and valleys, with scattered villages throughout. Still further west was the breath-taking Otohosk Sea, lining the entire coast of Majadon.

Now one day in the village of Bergen, a fair baby was born to parents who loved her more than treasure. Anya wasn't their first baby, but she was their first girl. In fact, she was the firstborn girl in their family for three generations.

Her older brothers, Garth and Günter, were the only ones who weren't happy she was a girl. They didn't yet know how wonderful girls were.

Anya's eyes were large and hazel green, and her hair the color of golden toast. She was given all the things babies need. And as babies go, she was good natured, if she was not left alone long during the day. Mama and Papa did all they could to assure her of their love.

But a problem arose. Once she started walking, she got into everything. Unpredictable and dangerous things. She couldn't be trusted farther than the road, and if nobody was watching, she'd wander. She loved the outdoors; it was her playground. She ate bugs, tied worms in knots, and left open the gates to the chicken coop or pigpen. She was fearless and would pet almost any animal.

She attempted to climb three garden trellises,

 and broke all of them. Ladders didn't scare her, neither the barn one nor the ladder to the roof, where Papa was making repairs. But water was what she loved most. Twice, Papa saved her from drowning when they

had picnics at the lake. Another time, he rescued her from falling in the well.

Indoors wasn't much better. She pulled dishes from shelves, unraveled yarn, or played in Mama's sewing basket. She cut her little brother's hair to bits with scissors. She got into boxes and trunks without permission. Once she played with Garth's slingshot, and snapped herself in the eye. It was black and blue for weeks.

But she grew out of that stage, and settled down. She became tired of the punishment for her behavior. She learned her chores and was good at them. She swept and dusted, fed the animals, gathered eggs, carried water inside, and helped Mama do laundry. This was good, for by now, she was needed more than ever to help.

Freya Tamarkin was a devoted mother who did everything she could to keep her family happy. She was especially busy these days caring for new baby Katia. Anya no longer was the only girl, nor Garth and Günter the only boys. Frederick arrived two years before Katia, and was even naughtier than Anya had been. So between Katia and Freddie, Mama depended on Anya.

Katia cried often in the night and woke everyone up. She was better during the day, but cranky until her milk digested. Anya and Günter took turns babysitting. They fed her, changed her nappies and on warm days, pushed her in the baby pram. But only Anya played the flute and when she did, Katia and Freddie would go to sleep.

Sometimes Mama gave her and Günter krones for helping, when she could spare it from the money she earned, doing laundry for rich villagers.

They saved their krones. Gunter wanted a bow and arrow. But Anya wanted to buy a gray donkey with a white face. A donkey could take her on exciting adventures.

There were no schools in Bergen. Most of the children's schooling came from Grandmama, who

lived down the road. They did four lessons a week, in the mornings. Grandmama didn't have enough strength to teach all day. Anya was glad, for that meant she could do her chores in the afternoons, and play before suppertime.

Gaillard Tarmarkin was a tradesman, selling his wares along the hard, rutted roads of the land. He made things from wood and metal, things to sit on and things to hang on walls like shelves and coat racks. Sometimes his things sold well. When they didn't, he'd be gone for days, to peddle them. The farthest village took a day to reach by wagon. When he traveled to Majadonia, he'd be gone even longer.

There were wild animals in the woods, brown bears and red foxes, deer and wolves, red squirrels and hedgehogs, shrews and birds . . . so many birds. Papa would take Anya for walks in Enchanted Forest, just the two of them. He always took his rifle and hunting knife along. He told her to never go there alone, whether day or night, that sometimes Yut the Defiant's forces would trespass there. His fort and campground were located in Shadow Forest, beyond the river, farther east.

Papa's words of warning rang in her ears, "Remember, Anya. Never go into the forest or swim in the river without a grownup. Do you hear me?" She remembered his stern face as he spoke these words.

Garth and Günter looked out for the younger ones while Papa was away. If Garth went with Papa, Günter guarded them on his own. He was not as strong or smart as Garth, but he was kind.

CHAPTER TWO

One day when Papa left on a trip, Anya finished her chores, and went for a walk along the Rusakov. She had played her flute, and Katia and Freddie were sleeping. She knew she couldn't go swimming. She looked for a place to sit down.

She stared at the river's dark blue surface, sparkling in the sun. The river was wide and deep. Many rocks and boulders lined its shores. Anya climbed one. As she reached the top, she was startled to see a boy sitting on a nearby rock, now in plain view. She waved to him.

He moved closer. He said this was his favorite spot. And that he lived in the village just north of Bergen.

"In Gieben? My father knows someone there, and my brother sells eggs there. What's your name? I'm Anya Tamarkin."

"Maxim Popyrin, but people call me Max."

They sat there, looking up river. He told her about his sisters; the older one was Nadja. The younger was a baby, only Danica was the opposite of Katia. She was crabby all day, and slept through the night.

As they spoke, the wind began to blow hard. It rippled the water and lapped at the rocks. The ripples turned to waves. A noise made Anya turn around. She looked downstream.

Something wiggled and poked out of the water. Circular ripples fanned out from it.

"Max, look! Was that a tail?"

He barely looked in time to see it go under the water.

They heard a long shrill, from the same direction. And squeals. They weren't threatening, instead the sounds seemed to beckon them.

They kept watching. What looked like a head rose above the water. It squealed, loudly.

Max's eyes met Anya's. "So that's what's making those noises!"

Anya gripped Max's arm. Max shuddered. They strained to see more. But a mist rose up.

Whatever was there was veiled. *Was the mist a fog, or the creature's breath?*

Things darkened. Anya looked skyward. As if by magic, a blanket of gray clouds formed. The wind turned cold.

She shivered. "Let's get out of here, Max." They scrambled off the rocks. He turned toward Gieben, and she to Bergen. She climbed the hill leading to the field behind her house.

At the top, she turned around. What she saw made her stand still. A creature hobbled out from the boulders where they'd been sitting, and lumbered onto the shore. It seemed to be in a hurry, or perhaps it stumbled. It lost

its balance and toppled over. With its wings folded under itself and legs wiggling in the air, it looked like an upended turtle. Anya forgot her fright and laughed. Its body rolled to one side, then the other. At last, it upended itself and stood up. It shook itself all over like dogs do, after they're soaked in water. Anya laughed again.

She didn't know if she should run home. She didn't want to hide. The animal headed toward her hill. But when it caught her eye, it stopped. It didn't make angry noises, so she thought if she stayed her distance, she'd be safe. She wanted a better look, and inched a little closer. The creature did the same. As she approached it more, Anya could identify it. A dragon! She thought dragons had ridges down their backs. This one didn't. She wasn't sure what it might do next.

Anya was a brave girl, but not that brave. She froze.

"Wowwwwg," said the dragon. Its voice was not loud, more like a purr. It lowered its head, and repeated its greeting.

Anya couldn't resist. She walked closer, now a stone's throw away. She'd heard stories about dragons, how some were evil, but others were kind and smart. Though feeling timid, she forced herself to lean in. "Dragon? Are you friend or foe?"

"Wowwwwg," it said again. Slowly its tail wagged left, then right. It bowed its head. Its eyes were large and emerald green. It made new noises, sweet noises.

Anya remained where she was.

"I'm a friend!" said the dragon.

Anya fell to the ground. "You can TALK? You're a talking dragon?"

"Well, of course! Have you not heard King Gregory has talking animals in his army? I guard the middle villages. Majadon's in a state of high alert right now. Spring is dangerous in the kingdom. Yut the Defiant's on the prowl for babies. He uses Siberian tigers to snatch them when their families and king's dragons are not vigilant."

"But why?"

"So he can train them in his evil ways, before they learn about Good. He cannot create things, but he can transform them. He needs human babies for his mission."

The dragon shook its head from side to side, and made a soft blowing sound, "Pfffft! Pfffft!" Its face looked kind of sad.

"Can't you stop Yut?" She knew babies disappeared from time to time in the villages. She'd heard Mama and Papa talk late at night when they thought she was sleeping. But she didn't know about any Siberian tigers. What were they?

"He won't get away with this for long. King Gregory will act soon."

"But what's the king's plan? How will he catch Yut and his army?"

The dragon's eyes twinkled. "I'll know soon. I'm not fast on land. But I swim and fly very well. And dragons have extremely strong jaws."

"Can you breathe fire?"

"When I'm in battle, or when danger appears. Never on a whim, or to show off."

Anya no longer felt uneasy. She asked the dragon if she could come closer.

"Come," Dragon said softly.

Anya stepped gingerly at first and circled the dragon, step over step. She studied its scaly body. Its coat was iridescent, a maroon-purple, its feet

lime green with dark claws. It was taller than a grown brown bear. Though she'd never seen a bear herself, Papa said their shoulders were as high as his chest. Its folded wings looked strong, and were streaked with green lines, just like its back.

She stopped beside the dragon's head and spoke. "May I pet you?"

Dragon nodded. Anya reached out slowly, put her hand on its shoulder, and petted gently. The scales did not permit her to pet upward, only downward. She moved her hand down its back, went under its outstretched wings, and walked to the tip of its tail. Its end had a hook, above and below.

She returned to the dragon's face. "I love your dark purple skin, Dragon. Do you have a name?"

"Oh yes, Queen Sasha names all the animals. I'm Vera. My two brothers help guard Majadon, too. Vicente watches the northern villages, and Vladimir the south. I guard the middle ones. Do you live in Bergen?"

"Yes. And Max lives in Gieben."

"I watch over his village also. Was Max the boy with you? Where did he go?"

"Yes. After we saw your tail, the sky turned dark. We started for home."

"As you should," said Vera. Your parents might worry. Hurry along, Anya. Don't be frightened of me. I'm your friend. I guard your house and Max's, and all of the middle villages. We'll meet again soon."

"Wait, how is it you called me Anya? I didn't tell you my name."

"King Gregory teaches his dragons all the people names."

"I see." Anya put her arms around Vera's head and hugged. When she stepped back, Vera licked her head and arms with her dry, scratchy tongue. Her breath smelled like wintergreen. Her tongue felt tickly and made Anya laugh.

She hurried home to tell Mama and Papa about Vera. Papa sat her down and told her about Yut. It seems that eons ago, Yut tried to de-throne King Gregory. He was thrown from the castle, and sent to Shadow Forest. There he was to live confined, with all his cohorts. He was commanded to leave all of Majadon alone.

She had a lot to tell Max the next time she saw him.

Surely King Gregory wouldn't allow evil to go on much longer in Majadon.

CHAPTER THREE

Anya didn't return to the river for weeks. Father had become ill with fever, chills and bouts of dizziness. Mother was so busy caring for him, Anya watched Katia even more. She couldn't go to Grandmama's for school, nor play, nor go for walks. But at night, she heard the same sweet shrill noises from the direction of the river. She was sure it was Vera. She played her flute at the window, and Vera would call back to her.

One day she was feeding Katia in her highchair while Mother hung the wash on the line. There came a knock at the front door. She opened it to see a man with his boy. Her eyes grew large.

"Max! How did you know I lived here?" Anya smiled.

Max didn't smile back. He lowered his head.

The man spoke. "Good afternoon, little girl. I'm friends with Gaillard Tamarkin. Some neighbors told me he lives here. Is that right? Can I see him?" He was panting. His face was red.

Anya went for her mother. Papa was still weak and needed his strength to get well.

The man wrung his hands. "How do you do, madam? I'm Arman Popyrin. This is Max, my son. Your husband and I do business together. I've come to ask for your help. Our baby's missing—she was in her play crib outdoors when the dog began to bark. Nadja went to calm the dog, and when she turned around, Danika was gone!"

"Why, that's terrible! Come in, please—and catch your breath."

Anya was terrified. She thought of the Siberian tigers. Did one of them get Max's baby sister? Katia was on her hip. She held her closer.

When Mr. Popyrin sat down, Mama said, "Sir, do you think she could have wandered off?"

He said she was too little to climb out of her crib; it had to have been a snatching. He asked if his family could stay with them while he rode to Majadonia to tell the king.

Mama sent Anya to find Garth.

He was in the work shed. The minute he left to get Mr. Popyrin's family, Mama bid the man good-bye, "God go with you!" She told him if he traded horses along the way, he might reach Majadonia in a day. He cut loose faster than Anya had ever seen a man ride.

Günter returned breathless with the egg money. He saw the boy, and asked Anya privately if it was Max. But Max didn't notice Günter. He was sitting on the floor with his hands over his face. He began to sob. Anya went to him.

Günter pulled Mama to the side, and said he had something to tell her. "You better sit down." But the door opened and Garth came in with Mrs. Popyrin and Nadja. Günter hesitated.

"Go ahead, son. If you know something, you better tell us. All of us."

He swallowed. "I was a long ways off, but I saw Yut's soldiers kidnap a baby in Gieben! They used a paddy wagon with a tiger in it. The driver let it out, cracked a whip, and it ran behind a house and came back, with something dangling from its mouth. I yelled, and ran as fast as I could toward them. But the driver handed the baby to the passenger, locked the tiger back up, and took off faster than a mudslide. I couldn't stop them."

"That evil Yut and his Siberian tigers!" yelled Anya.

Max's mother wailed, "That was probably Danika! My baby!" She melted into a chair.

"There, there, Belle," Mother said. She put her arms around her. "King Gregory won't let this rest until he's rescued her. You'll see."

Günter was shivering. Mama wrapped a blanket around his shoulders.

"Günter, that was courageous. I'm proud of you, son. Thank you for trying to stop Yut's soldiers."

"Oh yes, Günter," said Mrs. Popyrin. "Thank you for trying to save Danika!"

They made the best of the evening, but no one had cheery thoughts. No one was hungry and no one slept soundly. The owls called mournfully for hours. Anya and Max lay on padded blankets on the parlor floor. But they couldn't sleep.

"Let's do something, Max." They plotted. "Let's leave in the morning before anyone's awake, and find Vera."

At dawn, they slipped out, and ran straight to Grandmama's house. Anya made up a story, to get Grandmama to go help Mama with Katia and Frederick all morning. She told her that Mama sent her and Max to bring some finished laundry to Geiben, and collect the money.

Their scheme worked. When Grandmama was out of sight, they headed for the river. Vera was easy to find. She was catching fish by slapping the water with her tail, and scaring them out of the water. They flew up into the air so high, it was a wonder they landed in her mouth at

all. If things hadn't been so urgent, Anya might have been amused.

"Vera, come over here!" Anya begged.

When Vera heard about the calamity, she began to move her wings. "Don't worry, dear ones. The king will know exactly what to do." The sight of Vera's body lifting into the sky was thrilling.

When Anya and Max returned, their mothers weren't pleased. They told them about Vera, posthaste. But as for Anya lying to Grandmama, Mama said there would be a punishment for that.

"Yes, Mama. I'm sor—" Anya halted. Some loud yelling in the backyard gripped them. They ran outdoors.

Grandmama was in great distress. Her face was pale. "Freya! Anya! The baby's gone!"

Anya thought this could not be true. But Mama's face also lost color, and her hand went to her throat.

"I was hanging up clothes and turned for just a moment when . . . when . . ." Grandmama's voice trailed off.

Mama burst into tears. She wailed louder than Belle had. Now it was Belle who comforted Mama.

Gradually, the wails of her mother and grandmother softened, and Anya heard shouting coming from the road.

Garth and Günter ran to see what it was. None of them could believe the news. The villagers said another baby had been snatched, a boy named Zukav. His cottage was across from Shadow Forest.

"We must do something, Mother!" Garth said. "Let me go to Majadonia immediately."

Anya touched his arm. "Garth? There's a faster way. Our guardian dragon just flew there with the news of Danika. Her two brothers are guarding the remaining villages. We can ask one of them to send a patrol dragon to the castle, and tell the king about Katia and Zukav."

"You've met these dragons?" Garth said.

"Only Vera," said Max. "But she told us about Vicente and Vladimir. I can help you find one of them, Garth."

Garth and Max left before Mama could object.

Günter stood there with a forlorn look. "Why am I the last one asked to help?"

"You've done enough for one day, my son. You were an eye witness to a snatching, and told us about it. That was good. Don't trouble yourself further."

"Yes, Günter—and protecting us while Garth's away is important." Anya smiled. She waited for Mama to leave the room to ask him what he thought about conniving a way to rescue the babies from Yut's campground.

Later, Anya heard Vera calling her from beyond the back field. She went to her.

"Anya! Good news! King Gregory's planning a battle against Yut if he doesn't repent and surrender the babies. It'll take place soon. First, he must notify the villages with his messengers."

"But, Vera! Two more babies were kidnapped while you were gone! My sister Katia and Zukav, a boy baby. I just know Katia's crying for Mama and Papa. I can't even think about it. Poor Katia! Poor babies!"

Anya couldn't help herself. She began to cry.

"Now, now, Anya, hush. Stop crying. All is well. When Queen Sasha learned about the snatchings, she sent her Spirit dragon. Santo cast a spell of serenity upon the infants. They are no longer scared, or aware of danger. They're sleeping. Soon they'll be home; you'll see."

"Oh Vera, really? Thank you! I must tell the mamas. They'll be so happy."

But they didn't tell Papa. He was still weak and needed his strength to get well.

CHAPTER FOUR

King Gregory did just as Vera said. He sprang into action. First, he alerted all of Majadon that Yut was being confronted with an edict: relinquish the babies, or come under attack. Secondly, he announced that reconciliation with Yut would be sought. If that failed, all the able-bodied men of Majadon were to report in three days to Yut's compound in Shadow Forest, at dawn.

He sent his emissary to Yut's compound to deliver the injunction. Zahran demanded the babies be relinquished, but told Yut if he complied, his life and army would be spared.

Yut wasn't swayed. He denied that he even had the infants. But spies had seen the babies. Zahran knew he wasn't telling the truth. Yut spit on the ground and raised his fist. He commanded Zahran to vacate Shadow Forest at once. He smirked and bragged that he'd set his tigers loose, if they didn't leave quickly.

Zahran answered, "Yut, you know you violated the king's orders to live within the confines of Shadow Forest, and leave Majadon's inhabitants alone. You've flagrantly trespassed. Therefore, I give you this final message: In the name of King Gregory, I warn you, Yut. If you don't release the babies in three days, you and your hosts will perish from the face of the earth."

Yut roared with laughter. "Get out of here *now*

Zahran, and take your threats with you! I'm not afraid. My army's twice the size of the king's."

Zahran said no more. Behind him, he heard the voice of his men, mumbling. Some had drawn their swords when Yut defamed King Gregory.

"Men, put away your weapons," Zahran directed. Let us reserve our strength for the coming battle."

They reluctantly but obediently rode out of Shadow Forest for their three-day wait.

No one thought Yut would change his mind, but everyone worried what he might do before the battle. Mama and Grandmama worried. Mrs. Popryin worried. And Garth had to calm Zukav's family for their fears.

Anya thought three days was too long to wait. She wanted to save Katia before the battle began. She planned a way to rescue the babies in the darkness of the night. She would get girls from Bergen and Gieben to come along, in two wagons. Günter would drive one, and Garth the other. Sleeping dust made of passion flower and valerian root could be used on the tigers, making them nod off. Garth could open a nursery window and Anya, who was small enough to climb in, could sneak the babies out, one by one. The girls would carry and hold the babies in the back of the wagon as they escaped, safe and sound. Of course, Max would ride on the end of the last wagon, toting a sword.

But that night, a heavy sleep fell upon Anya, Max and her brothers. They saw Queen Sasha's dragon, Santo. He sent the same dream to each of them. In it, the Rusakov River was before them, and a mist rose up. Out of the mist, Vera's head rose from the water, and she swam to them. Vicente and Vladimir flew in, and hovered beside her.

"Fear not," the three dragons said, in unison. "The babies are sleeping and safe. They shall be rescued on the day of battle. If you try now, all of you will be caught. Wait for King Gregory. You'll see. When you awake, you'll have peace."

And when they awoke, they did.

Garth and Günter went to fight along with the village men and the king's army. Papa would not know of it now, but Mama sent them with her prayers. Anya and Max snuck out that afternoon to watch the battle preparations. They hid in the forest bushes, quiet as dormice.

The villagers brought food and water. The men bided their time, sharpened their knives, and practiced the battle plan for the oncoming siege, taking turns sleeping. There was talking and praying and much nervous laughter.

CHAPTER FIVE

O n the morning of the battle, Anya and Max ran to a new hiding spot to watch. They found a tree on a knoll overlooking Yut's fort. Its branches were low lying, and they hid beneath them. The king's dragons arrived—fuchsia, green, orange and dark blue ones. Upon the largest dragon, red with silver wings and feet, rode the king. His garb was regal—his topcoat pure white and his breeches, purple. He was armed with scepter, sword, and helmet. A glow of light circled his face.

Anya and Max were silent, their eyes transfixed on him.

The ground rumbled as King Gregory assembled his army outside the parameter of Yut's compound. All the soldiers and village men on foot, horse, oxen or dragons held their backs erect, confident of victory. The king went before them, and brandished his sword.

King Gregory faced the fort's tall iron doors. "Yut! We've come for the children. Relinquish them now and no one will be harmed, neither you nor your army!"

There came no reply. From inside the fort, a putrid green smoke rose from its center and billowed upwards. It smelled of sulfur. Within this smoke, Yut and his legions were hoisted above the fort walls on the wings of birdlike creatures. They hovered three deep in a line that stretched from one side of the fort to the other.

Anya and Max gasped. She imagined that even the bravest man would tremble, seeing this fearsome scene. The dazzling, oversized birds were so shimmery and bright, Anya and Max shielded their eyes. Though similar in body to giant lizards, their coats were not dull in color, but gold, silver or bronze. Some were navigated by their riders to go back and forth in the front line, threateningly.

"Drominites!" said King Gregory. "He's called drominites into his service! Don't be afraid of those flying lizards!"

Nevertheless, the village fighters took off running for cover, to the forest. But the king's army and dragons were trained and obedient. They stood their ground, awaiting his next command.

In a loud voice, he told them that drominites were flawed: they needed sunlight to fly, and were swift moving only if they had a rider. Without light, they fell to the ground. And without a rider, they lost power and had to fly low, vulnerable to arrows.

"Villagers! Back into position! Make ready your arrows and spears! You're about to see the power of Good before your very eyes!" They ran back, and took up their posts.

"Prepare for battle! Those in the rear, prepare your bows! Those in front and center, raise your swords and knifes for hand to hand combat!"

He raised his scepter to the blazing sun. The clouds rushed to cover it. Caught off guard, some drominites crashed to the ground, one or two at a time. The rest could only glide near the ground, making for easy targets. Dazed and disoriented, the downed riders couldn't remove their weapons quickly, and were captured with nets. The remaining airborne warriors threw spears at the king's soldiers. In the rear, the village men provided archery support.

Max was mesmerized by the battle. Anya put her face to the ground, "I can't look! Is it going well?"

Max paid her no heed. She raised her voice and tugged his leg. "*Max*, is it going well?"

"Yes, Anya. Look! Yut's men are falling like dead wasps!"

But suddenly, the doors of the fort opened, and tigers came out growling and baring their teeth. What remained of Yut's army cheered.

The king's soldiers stepped back. King Gregory pointed his scepter at the tigers. They froze.

Turning around, he called his dragons, "Dragons! Attack!" He tapped his scepter, and the tigers came back into action.

Max said, "Anya, there's Vera and her brothers! They're flying at the tigers!"

Anya looked. The dragons were gripping the tigers by their necks. Their jaws snapped the tigers' necks like twigs. Death was instant.

But Vera was in peril: she couldn't get a grip on a tiger's neck. It broke loose and turned on her. It clawed her nose. Vera fell to the ground. The tiger circled her body. Anya was certain it wanted to get to her throat.

"V E R A!" shrieked Anya. Ignoring the danger of the ongoing battle, she ran headlong down the hill to help. Vera had fallen into a copse of trees, partly removed from the fighting.

Max followed her.

CHAPTER SIX

When Anya screamed Vera's name the second time, King Gregory turned around. He aimed his scepter at the tiger. It froze.

"Vera! Oh Vera!" cried Anya, now at her side. She took her head in her lap, and stroked the dragon's forehead. Max watched, at their side.

King Gregory rode over and waved his scepter. "Vera of Majadon, arise!"

Vera awoke, stood up, and shook her head. A twinkling white dust swept across her face, and the blood around her nose vanished.

Anya and Max clapped their hands and jumped for joy. King Gregory aimed his scepter at the tiger, and tapped it. The giant cat regained its mobility.

"Breathe fire, Vera!" he commanded.

A stream of fire poured from her mouth. When the smoke cleared, only ashes remained.

Anya and Max ran back to their lookout. A flash of something caught Max's eye. He looked left, and saw a dare devilish figure standing on the tower ledge, his fist raised.

"Anya, look! That must be Yut!" Neither she nor Max had ever seen Yut. They gasped.

The man scowled at the dead and defeated legion. He signaled to something inside the fort. A huge brown and burnt-orange dragon with spikes along its spine flew to him. He mounted the grotesque creature. They turned away from the king.

King Gregory called, "Yut the Defiant!"

Yut's foreboding creature spun around, and flew at the king with a hiss. Fire streamed from its mouth in a long line. The king raised his shield.

When the fire hit, it turned to mist. King Gregory directed his scepter to Yut and his dragon.

He commanded the hovering dragon, "No longer shall you oppose the Good forces of this kingdom, Anticles!"

He addressed Yut next. "No longer shall you commit evil in the land of Majadon, Yut! The fire you have used shall turn upon your head."

King Gregory motioned his dragons forward without taking his eyes off Yut and Anticles.

"Dragons! Breathe!" The dragons surrounded Yut and Anticles. Fire spewed from their mouths. The fire was quick and all-consuming. And then, it was over. When the dragons backed away, nothing but twinkling sparks filled the air, floating and falling to the ground. The dead were burned, the tigers re-located to a far-away territory, and the drominites re-trained as king's agents. Yut's survivors were given the chance to repent and labor in chains. If they worked for King Gregory, their prison cells had windows, although barred ones. They received three meals a day. If they declined service, they went to dungeons, whereupon they got porridge at noon and soup at night.

At the king's orders, Garth and Günter brought out the babies. One by one, they were haltered to a dragon and flown home. Zukav was delivered by Vladimir and Max held Danika, on Vicente. Anya papoosed Katia to her back, and they rode Vera.

That evening, Papa sat up in bed, saying he was feeling better. "Freya, where's my five beloved children?"

"Home," Mama said, "thanks to King Gregory Defender of Men and Queen Sasha the Watchful." She put Katia in his arms.

Garth and Günter would soon tell Papa about the battle for Good. When all his strength returned.

After that day, there was never evil again in beautiful Majadon.

Almost.

But at least no babies were kidnapped. No Siberian tigers or drominites returned, and no servants of the king defected. Everyone lived in peace.

Soon thereafter, a little gray donkey with a white face appeared in the Tamarkin's yard, tied to the fence. From its neck hung a scroll strung with a red silk cord.

To Anya and her family,

For bravely fighting evil in Majadon.

K. G.

GLOSSARY AND CHARACTERS

all-consuming, adj. Completely taken over.

Anticles (Ăn′ tĭ cleez), *n.* Fearless, fire-breathing dragon of Yut the Defiant, largest in Majadon.

Anya (Ŏn′ ya)**Tamarkin** (Tah mar′ kin), *n.* First born girl in Tamarkin family for three generations. The main character of this book and the series.

Arman (Ar′ mahn) **Popyrin** (Pop′ ă rĭn), *n.* Father of Max, Nadja and Danika; lives in Gieben with family.

Belle (Bĕll) **Popyrin**, *n.* Wife of Arman Popyrin, Max's mother.

beloved, adj. An old expression for loved very much.

Bergen (Bŭr′ gĕn), *n.* A city in mid Majadon; population 10,777. Home of Gaillard Tamarkin and family.

Bodo (Bō′ dō), *n.* Newest and most northern city of Majadon; population 4,126.

brandished, v. To wave one's sword in a defiant or showy way.

commit, v. To do, to put into motion and complete.

copse, n. A small group of trees.

declined, v. To refuse, to say no, to go without.

defect, v. Leave a cause or country to join an opposing one.

Danika (Dŏn' ĭ ka), *n.* Youngest girl of the Popyrin's, who is kidnapped.

Drammend (Dră' mund), *n.* First city north of Majadonia, on the King's highway. Population 11,116.

Drominite (Drom' ĭ nite), *n.* Cousin to the dragon, without fire-breath. Body: eight feet, tail: six feet; spikes on spine and tail; legs strong and birdlike, with claws. Reptilian origin; lays eggs.

dungeon (dun' gən), *n.* A windowless prison, underground, musky, clay-smelling, damp, dark.

emissary, *n.* Messenger or servant sent on a mission.

Enchanted Forest, *n.* The long stretch of thick forest that covers most of Majadon, starting near Majadonia and extending to Bodo and beyond. Inhabited by countless mammals, birds and yet-to-be discovered creatures. Home to hundreds of Maja-don's cottages. Off limits to Yut.

Frederick (Freddie) Tamarkin, *n.* Fourth born child; Anya's youngest brother.

Freya (Frāy′ yu)**Tamarkin**, *n.* Anya' mother.

haltered, *v.* Tied up in a supportive way around the chest.

Gaillard Tamarkin, *n.* Anya's father.

Garth Tamarkin, *n.* Anya's oldest brother, the first-born boy.

Gieben (Gē′ bĕn), *n.* Twin city of Bergen, ½ mile north. Population 8,815. Home of Arman Popyrin's family.

Grandmama (Gran ma ma′), *n.* Mother of Freya Tamarkin, maternal grandmother.

Günter (Gün′ terr), *n.* Anya's oldest brother, the second born boy.

hovering, *v.* To be suspended in air.

injunction, *n.* A command, order or directive.

iridescent, *adj.* A rainbow display of color, lustrous.

Katia Tamarkin, *n.* Newborn baby of family, Anya's sister.

King Gregory Defender of Men, *n.* The great ruler of Majadon; fights for justice and righteousness in the kingdom; has a magical scepter.

The King's Highway, *n.* A two-lane hard packed dirt and stone road leading from Majadonia to Bodo, and beyond; guarded by the king's army night and day.

knoll, *n.,* a small, rounded hill.

legion, n. A large group or army.

Majadon (mâ′ sja-don), a fantasy kingdom located approximately 60.4720° N of the equator and 8.4689° E of the prime meridian. Upon a parcel of land measuring 148,738 square miles, its northern boundaries are largely unexplored.

Majadonia (mâ sja don′ ya), *n.* Capital city of Majadon, located at the southern tip of the Rusakov River, as it enters the Otohosk Sea. Population 21,948. Home of the Majadon Castle.

Maxim Popyrin, *n.* Friend of Anya, fellow fighter of evil, lives in Geiben; nicknamed Max.

mobility, adj. Ability to move freely.

Nadja (Nŏd′ jah), *n.* First born child of Arman and Belle Popyrin, Max's oldest sister.

North Sea, *n*. The larger body of water to Majadon's west; its western boundaries unknown.

navigate, *v*., to control the course and position of a flying machine.

Otohosk (Ō′ tō hŏsk) **Sea**, *n*. Channel between the Majadon peninsula and the southern continent; navigable by ship or boat.

papoosed, *v*. Tied to another person or animal's body.

patrol dragon, *adj*. & *n*. A support dragon of King Gregory, good at protecting humans.

Queen Sasha the Watchful, *n*. Kind wife of King Gregory. Has ability to see into the hearts of her subjects and bring them comfort.

Rusakov (Rūs′ ka hŏv) **River**, *n*. Majadon's longest river winding through Enchanted Forest from Bodo down to Majadonia, emptying into the Otohosk Sea. Wild and raging in parts.

Santo (Săn′ to), *n*. Spirit Dragon of Queen Sasha who does her bidding; can enter dreams and thoughts of humans and animals.

scepter (sĕp′ ter), *n*. An ornamental wand held by a person with ruling authority; King Gregory's held magical powers; shorter than a meter.

Shadow Forest, *n.* The far eastern section of Enchanted Forest where Yut and his army reside.

Siberian tigers, *n.* Agents of Yut; trained kidnappers of Majadon babies.

tradesman, *n.* A crafts person or someone engaged in the selling of wares.

unknown territory, *n.* Land not explored or well known by Majadonians, though inhabited. A few of its residents took homes in Majadon, in the woods. It borders Majadon's western border, and continues to its northernmost tip, and west.

Valerian, *n.* A plant of the genus Valeriana, with fragrant pink or white flowers cultivated for use as a medicinal sedative.

Vera, (Věr′ a) *n.* The female dragon of the king whom Anya meets first. Guards the middle kingdom of Majadon; can swim and fly skillfully, not graceful on land.

Vicente (Vī sent′ tay), *n.* The brother of Vera who guards northern Majadon.

Vladimir, (Vläd′ ĭ meer), *n.* Another brother of Vera who guards southern Majadon.

"Wowwwwg," *n.* A greeting; dragon language for 'Hello! How do you do?"

Yut's Campground, *n.* Fort and residence of Yut and his army.

Yut (Yŭt) **the Defiant**, *n.* Former servant of King Gregory who rebelled; was sent to Shadow Forest for the rest of his days.

Zahran (Ză′ răn), *n.* Emissary of King Gregory. Also his right-hand servant.

Zukav (Sū′kof), n. A boy baby from a cottage near Shadow Forest who is kidnapped.

ABOUT THE AUTHOR

Deborah Thomas has authored children's songs and poems her entire teaching career. Writing and illustrating a children's story is a dream come true. *The Battle of Shadow Forest* is her first fairy tale in the series *Anya of Majadon.*

Born in Grand Rapids, Michigan, she enjoyed small town community life and spent summers at Big Lake, surrounded by farms. She recently bought a getaway house nearby, in Allegan, to return to that lifestyle, when possible.

Graduated from the University of Arizona in 1970, she taught elementary school almost thirty years. Upon retiring, she became a substitute and piano teacher. Re-married in 2000, she's the mother of two pair of loving daughters and stepdaughters and a happy grandmother to eleven grandchildren. She and her husband recently adopted a rescue puppy, naming her Pippa.

ACKNOWLEDGMENTS

I want to acknowledge the following for the indispensable contribution they made to this book. Without them, this story could not have unfolded or been written free of error.

Interior layout, KDP technician, and back cover, Benjamin Vrbicek

Graphic artist & book cover, Monty Kugler

Illustrations, Deborah Thomas

Mentor & KDP introduction, Scott Combs

Prayer that I would grow up with an imagination, Dorothy Thomas Moffet, my mother

Professional readers: Victoria Bergesen, Marcia Cook Dorman, Elizabeth Goodman, Julie Eberhardt, Karen A. Kirkland, Julie Maniglia, Lisa Periale Martin & Kathy Wimbish

Endorsements: Lisa Periale Martin & Kathy Wimbish

Writing instructor, Professor Meg Files, Pima College, Tucson who challenged her students to enter writing contests, experience rejection & improve their skills

Made in the USA
Monee, IL
26 August 2019